To Rich, Alexa, and Grace, for all your
love, encouragement, and belief that
I could do this . . .

From strawberries to sawdust and all the
smells that made the memories I still cherish
today: may those who read this little story
allow their senses to become more alive to
the world around them . . . (sniff sniff).

www.mascotbooks.com

It Smells Like Tuesday

For more information, please contact:
Mascot Books
620 Herndon Parkway, Suite 320
Herndon, VA 20170
info@mascotbooks.com

Library of Congress Control Number: 2020919146

CPSIA Code: PRT1220A
ISBN-13: 978-1-64543-290-6

Printed in the United States

It Smells Like Tuesday

Amy Provinzono-Thomas   Illustrated by Bryan Janky

Tyler loved to smell things.

He loved the smell of his new crayons on the first day of school.

He loved to tease his sister and chase her all around the house to sniff his stinky shoes!

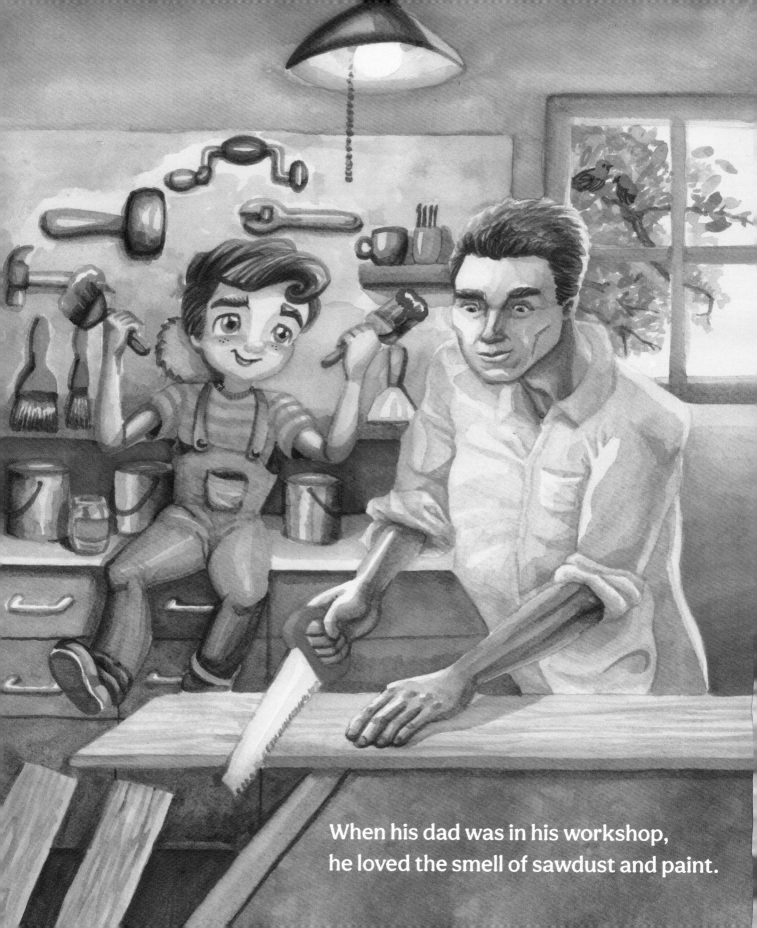

When his dad was in his workshop,
he loved the smell of sawdust and paint.

When he visited Grandma's house, the air smelled of chocolate chip cookies.

That always made Tyler hungry!

When he hugged his mom, he loved
the faint smell of her rose perfume.

Tyler never wanted to forget the smells he loved! So, he bottled them in little jars and kept them neatly lined up on a shelf in his room. His collection had many great scents...

He collected clippings of freshly cut grass.

He bottled sand and ocean water
from his vacation at the beach.

He even put some half-chewed strawberry gum–his favorite flavor–in a jar.

The sense of smell was Tyler's superpower!

He could always predict a snowstorm just by smelling the air!

He knew the second his little sister Pyper needed her diaper changed and quickly reported it to someone in charge.

And…he even knew what was for lunch before his class got to the cafeteria each day at school!

On the first day of second grade, Tyler was chosen to be the line leader to the lunchroom. He took a whiff of the hallway air and happily announced,

"It Smells Like Tuesday!"

His teacher thought she misheard him and asked him to repeat what he had said. Once again, he reiterated that the air smelled like Tuesday.

Hmmm… thought his teacher. This young, Renaissance man sparked her curiosity. "What does Tuesday smell like, Tyler?"

Tyler's answer to his teacher's question was quite simple. He could hardly believe she could not answer it herself.

He gave her a wide-eyed look and hungry smile. "Tuesday smells like salsa, cheese, and taco shells!"

Once Tyler and his class reached the warm cafeteria with students bustling in line with their trays and loudly chatting at tables, his prediction was confirmed.

It indeed was Tuesday, that was undoubtedly true, and Tyler was right–tacos were being served!

Tyler was quite happy as a delicious tray of tacos were plated up just for him! Tacos were his favorite; his nose and super-power sniffer had not failed him again.

Then, once he was seated with his friends, he took out one of his little jars from his pocket, opened the lid, and swept the jar excitedly through the cafeteria air. He closed the lid quickly and tightly as to not lose the smell and labeled the outside: "TACO TUESDAY!" He had another jar of one of his favorite smells to add to the collection on his bedroom shelf.

As Tyler savored each delicious bite of his taco lunch, he wondered what new, interesting smells he would encounter the rest of the day...

Did You Know?

- People can detect at least one trillion smells.

- You can smell fear and disgust.

- The sense of smell is the oldest sense. (Chemodetection is the detection of chemicals related to smell or tastes and is the most ancient sense.)

- Women have a better sense of smell than men.

- Dogs have nearly 44 times more scent cells than humans. Humans have five to six million odor-detecting cells compared to dogs, who have 220 million cells. It is said that we have evolved to rely less on our sense of smell, while most animals have retained it.

- Like fingerprints, every person has their own, distinct odor.

- Our olfactory bulb has direct connections to two brain areas that are strongly connected to emotion and memory—the amygdala and hippocampus. No other sense passes through these brain areas.

- It has been said that people who are exposed to the smells of baking cookies and roasted coffee are more inclined to help a stranger. Whereas, when in a foul-smelling place, one becomes more anxious, aggressive, and angry.

How About a Little "Smell" Talk?

1. My favorite smell is _____.

2. The smell of _____ reminds me of _____.

3. The smelliest smell I ever sniffed was _____.

4. I love the smell of _____ cooking in the kitchen.

5. When I think of my favorite season, the smell of _____ comes into my mind.

Amy P. Thomas is a military wife and the mother of two beautiful daughters, Alexa and Grace. She has been a teacher for the last thirty-one years and is also a blogger. She lives in Paoli, Pennsylvania, with her family and her dog, Wilson.

Amy had a goal of writing a children's book for as long as she could remember. *It Smells Like Tuesday* was born from an actual experience of leading a group of second graders to the cafeteria one day and having a "smelly" conversation with one of the students leading the line.

Her message is quite simple to all budding authors, young and old. She advises everyone to always look, listen, feel, and SMELL the world around them. Wake up your senses, for there are endless stories waiting to be told. She says you can do anything you set your mind to by following your dreams, working hard, and being persistent.